Always for Bill —JS

To Sweet, Sweet Jackie —BS

fLeas!

JEANNE STEIG

Illustrated by BRITT SPENCER

PHILOMEL BOOKS

erfect, perfect, perfect!" said Quantz. "Not a cloud in the sky, not a weed to be seen." He hoed a bit, humming his favorite tune: "Patta pim, patta pum, the day has begun. Pitta pom, pitta posh—there's a dog in the squash!"

And so there was. A shaggy red dog had come by, and stopped for a scratch.

"Well, there you are," said Quantz, giving it a good rub behind the left ear, "and no extra charge." The dog galloped off, and Quantz discovered that he *had* been repaid, with a wonderful case of fleas.

He itched! He scratched his shoulder, his elbow itched; he scratched his elbow, the soles of his feet tormented him. Worst of all was the itch on his back, which was not within reach for scratching.

He threw down his hoe and ran to the road. "Please leave me alone, little critters," he implored. "You dance very well, but I can't abide it."

Down the road ran Quantz, looking for help. Sure enough, a woman was coming along with a man at her side, jabbering busily into her ear. "Please, miss," cried Quantz, "I'm beset by a terrible itching. Have you any advice?"

"In fact," said the woman, looking him over, "you have a first-rate case of fleas. I, on the other hand, am bedeviled by this impossible uncle, who never stops talking. I'd be happy to trade you."

"Fair enough and then some," said Quantz. "Fleas, fleas, move on if you please." The lady passed him the uncle, the fleas jumped onto her, and off she went, scratching away, while the uncle attached himself firmly to Quantz without losing a word.

"How nice," cried the uncle, "to be granted a change of companions, I've used up all of my nieces and nephews; they send me along from one to another, but that was the last one. You'll find I'm a real compendium: I can talk about anything. For example, I'll name every bone in your body. Tarsal, humerus, dactyl—"

"Dactyl?" asked Quantz.

"A bone in your foot. Or botany—look, there's a clingwort, lying in wait. If you touch it, it never lets go. Never."

Neither do uncles, thought Quantz.

"Mathematics!" exclaimed the uncle. "Zero times zero is—"

"Zero," said Quantz. It might have been wiser, he thought, to have stuck with fleas.

"Would you care for a song?" asked the uncle. "I have an inexhaustible repertoire: gloomy or frisky, wretched, romantic—" Just then a man came stumbling along with a huge chunk of Limburger cheese in his arms. "I say," said the uncle, interrupting himself, "you're heavily laden."

"I am," said the man. "I've a mountain of cheese, but never a friend in the world."

"Here's Uncle," cried Quantz. "He's surely the best companion a person could ask for. I'll do you the favor of swapping Uncle for that cumbersome Limburger cheese."

"Done, done!" said the man, and off they went, each happy with the bargain.

"Yum yummity yum," sang Quantz, and he nibbled a bit at his burden. But the sun beat down and the stinky cheese melted onto his sleeve and grew heavier every minute. "At least it's quiet," said he.

"Heigh-ho," sang a tiny voice. A trio of mice pulled up beside him, hauling a wagon in which lay a battered banjo. "Oh, cheese!" they whispered. "Oh, lovely Limburger cheese!"

"Do you like it?" asked Quantz.

"We're mad about it," replied the mice, sniffing it hungrily.

"I don't suppose you would care to swap your old banjo for this luxurious lump of cheese?" asked Quantz.

"Indeed, indeed," squealed the mice, capering gleefully, and the trade was quickly made.

"Strum strummity strum; I'll give it a try." Quantz plucked a few
strings, and a few strings more, but the notes were all a-jumble, and
his fingertips ached. "Not for me, that's evident," sighed Quantz.
"Let's see what turns up next. I'm doing a very brisk business."

Sure enough, a woman with wild red hair bounced down the road
toward him. "Dear madam," Quantz asked, "are you at all musical?"

"Ah," said she, "if only I had something as fine as your banjo. I'd
give the very hair on my head for it!" And to Quantz's amazement
she yanked off her hair, revealing a charming mop of blond curls
beneath it.

"Your wish is granted," said Quantz, with a bow.
And he plopped the wig onto his head, while the
woman set off with the banjo clutched tight in her arms.

"Wig jiggity jig," warbled Quantz, his blazing red hair on
display. But the wig grew too warm, so he pulled it off and
walked on, tossing it up and catching it. It wasn't long before a
man as bald as an apple appeared.

"A wig! What a glorious thingamajig!" the man exclaimed.
Quantz had no trouble at all persuading him to swap the wig for
the rabbit peering expectantly out of his pocket. "I found him asleep
by the side of the road, so I brought him along. You look like a
trustworthy lad, and I am greatly in need of that headpiece."

And he bent his head toward Quantz, who flipped the wig
neatly into place in exchange for the rabbit, which he put in
his own pocket.

"A dear little rabbit, chum chummity chum," he sang to himself. But the rabbit would not stay put; he popped up every two minutes, like a restless jack-in-the-box, with a powerful kick at Quantz's ribs. "I don't think he cares for me," said Quantz sadly. "Be patient, I beg of you. Somebody perfect will come along soon." And he continued on his way.

A long time went by till a fine-looking man in a shiny top hat appeared. He stopped dead in his tracks at the sight of Quantz with the rabbit out of his pocket, its front paws waving frantically. "A fine day to you and your rabbit," the man cried.

"Ah, yes," replied Quantz. "My rabbit. To tell you the truth, we are not the happiest couple on earth. He's a first-rate rabbit, but something is lacking between us. It's hard to explain." Now the rabbit was kicking furiously, and when Quantz pulled him out of his pocket, he leaped joyfully into the stranger's arms.

"You see how it is," said Quantz. "He's meant to be yours. You can give me whatever you like for him."

"My dear friend, I have nothing whatsoever to give. All I can offer is one bare bone, left over from last night's supper." And he pulled a bone from his pocket, bowed, and handed it over to Quantz.

"A bone. As bare as can be," said Quantz. "But the rabbit is happy, and that's worth something." The rabbit was nestling in the man's arms, twitching its nose with pleasure. So Quantz left them together, and set off again, "Botta bim, botta bum," down the road. "In the end," said he, "I've traded my fleas for a naked bone, but I suppose one could say that I've come off the better for it. I've had a fine walk and met many interesting folk. Perhaps I had best be content with the bargain and go back home."

He was just about to turn back when a little tent appeared before him, and guarding its door stood the very same dog who had given him fleas to begin with.

"No hard feelings," called Quantz, and sailed the bone into the air to prove it. The dog raced after it, and Quantz stepped into the tent.

"Look at that, will you!" cried Quantz. "A flea circus!" And there was the woman who had taken the fleas, presiding over their antics.

The tiny creatures danced graceful gavottes, fancy fandangos, and riotous rhumbas. They pulled miniature wagons, juggled, did high jumps and took breathtaking dives. The most daring of all was shot from a cannon and somersaulted back to a fine silver wire, where it tipped its almost invisible hat toward Quantz.

In the center of the tent the lonely man and the talkative uncle delivered a rollicking song together, while the woman with the banjo played lustily beside them. The bald man in his new red wig made a marvelous clown, and the mice, having chewed their great wheel of cheese into a labyrinth, ran and tumbled through it merrily.

Best of all were the man and his rabbit. What dizzying tricks the creature played! He vanished and reappeared in an instant, cavorted atop the red wig, and even spent a friendly moment in Quantz's pocket.

"Patta pim-pam-pun, what a barrel of fun!" cried Quantz. And he watched with glee till all the performers were finished and the tiny flea circus was packed up neatly in a matchbox. "Patta pim-pam-pome, it's time to head home," sang Quantz. "Patta pum, patta poo, would you like to come too?"

And back down the road he went, with the dog trotting briskly by his side, the bone in its mouth.

"I expect I'll be calling you Fleas," said Quantz. "Do you think that would suit you?"

The dog wagged his tail—and tipped up his head for a scratch.

Patricia Lee Gauch, editor

PHILOMEL BOOKS

A division of Penguin Young Readers Group.
Published by The Penguin Group.
Penguin Group (USA) Inc., 375 Hudson Street, New York, NY 10014, U.S.A.
Penguin Group (Canada), 90 Eglinton Avenue East, Suite 700, Toronto, Ontario M4P 2Y3, Canada
(a division of Pearson Penguin Canada Inc.).   Penguin Books Ltd, 80 Strand, London WC2R 0RL, England.
Penguin Ireland, 25 St. Stephen's Green, Dublin 2, Ireland (a division of Penguin Books Ltd).
Penguin Group (Australia), 250 Camberwell Road, Camberwell, Victoria 3124, Australia
(a division of Pearson Australia Group Pty Ltd).   Penguin Books India Pvt Ltd, 11 Community Centre, Panchsheel Park,
New Delhi - 110 017, India.   Penguin Group (NZ), 67 Apollo Drive, Rosedale, North Shore 0632, New Zealand
(a division of Pearson New Zealand Ltd).   Penguin Books (South Africa) (Pty) Ltd, 24 Sturdee Avenue, Rosebank,
Johannesburg 2196, South Africa.   Penguin Books Ltd, Registered Offices: 80 Strand, London WC2R 0RL, England.

Published simultaneously in Canada.   Manufactured in China by South China Printing Co. Ltd.

Design by Semadar Megged.   Text set in 15-point Italian Old Style.

The illustrations were done in mixed media including watercolor, gouache, and ink on Arches watercolor paper.
Library of Congress Cataloging-in-Publication Data

ISBN 978-0-399-24756-9
1 3 5 7 9 10 8 6 4 2